For A.M.B., keeper of dreams

Text copyright © 1984 by Harriet Ziefert.
Illustrations copyright © 1984 by Norman Gorbaty, Inc.
All rights reserved under International and Pan-American Copyright Conventions.
Published in the United States by Random House, Inc., New York, and simultaneously
in Canada by Random House of Canada Limited, Toronto. Originally published by
Random House, Inc., in 1984 as a Step into Reading® Book.

Library of Congress Cataloging-in-Publication Data
Ziefert, Harriet. Sleepy dog. SUMMARY: Simple text and illustrations portray a small
dog getting ready for bed, sleeping, dreaming, and waking up.
[1. Bedtime—Fiction. 2. Dreams—Fiction. 3. Night—Fiction. 4. Dogs—Fiction.]
I. Gorbaty, Norman, ill. II. Title. III. Series. PZ7.Z487SI 1984 [E] 84-4775
ISBN 0-394-86877-3 (pbk.) — ISBN 0-394-96877-8 (lib. bdg.)

Printed in the United States of America 10 9 8 7 6 5 4 3 2 1

GROLIER
BOOK CLUB EDITION

Sleepy Dog

by Harriet Ziefert
illustrated by Norman Gorbaty

A Bright & Early Book

From BEGINNER BOOKS
A division of Random House, Inc.

"Time for bed,
sleepyhead."

Sleepy, sleepy,
up to bed.

Head on pillow.
Nose under covers.
Cat on bed.

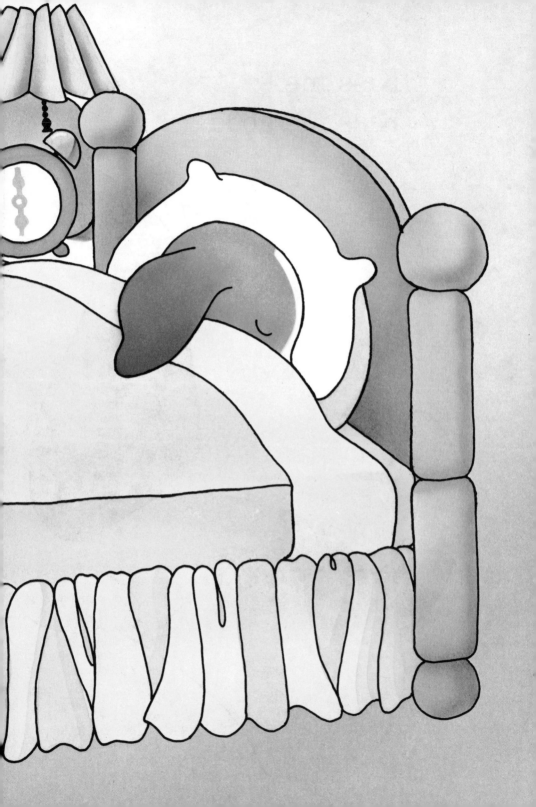

Kiss me.
Kiss me good.

Kiss me good night.

Turn on the moon.
Turn off the light.

Sleepy, sleepy,
sweet dreams tonight.

I dream
I am eating.

I dream
I am jumping.

I dream
I am running.

Someone is
chasing me.
HELP!

Now I am awake.

I need a drink
of water.

Sleepy, sleepy,
back to bed.

Tick, tick, tick, tick.
The clock says
tick, tick, tick, tick.

The clock shouts
ring, ring, ring!
Wake up!

Turn off the moon.

Turn on the sun.

Turn off the clock.

Turn on the light.

Good morning, cat...

time to play!

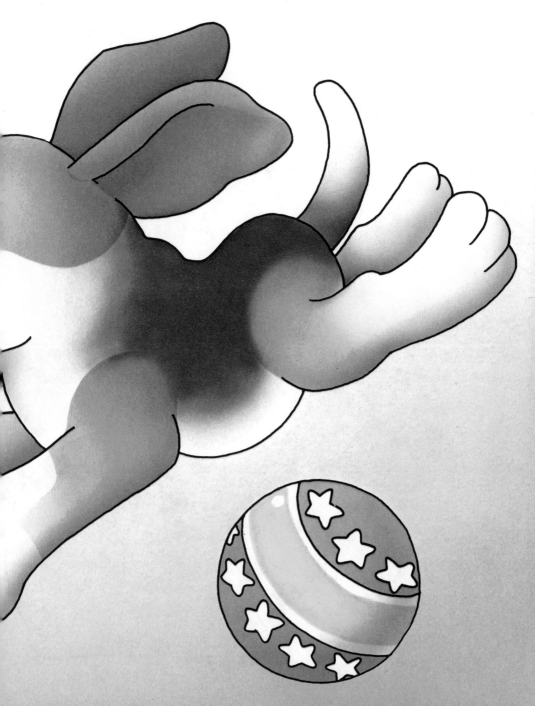

"Good morning,
little dog."

This Book Belongs to...

_____

© Illus. Dr. Seuss 1957